Cupid's Secret

For
William
with

Much Love

from
Dyida
Дїда = My Name
in the
Ukrainian Language
May 26, 2014
Monday
Seattle, Wa

Cupid's Secret

by Buck Kalinowski
illustrated by Kimberly Miller

Enjoy my book.
Buck

Printed in Victoria, Canada

Canadian Cataloguing in Publication Data

Kalinowski, Buck, 1958-
   Cupid's secret

   ISBN 1-55212-406-1

   1. Horses--Juvenile fiction. I. Miller, Kim. II. Title.
PZ7.K1415Cu 2000 j813'.6   C00-910808-4

TRAFFORD

This book was published *on-demand* in cooperation with Trafford Publishing.
On-demand publishing is a unique process and service of making a book available for retail sale to the public taking advantage of on-demand manufacturing and Internet marketing. **On-demand publishing** includes promotions, retail sales, manufacturing, order fulfilment, accounting and collecting royalties on behalf of the author.

Suite 6E, 2333 Government St., Victoria, B.C. V8T 4P4, CANADA
Phone   250-383-6864   Toll-free 1-888-232-4444 (Canada & US)
Fax   250-383-6804   E-mail   sales@trafford.com
Web site www.trafford.com TRAFFORD PUBLISHING IS A DIVISION OF TRAFFORD HOLDINGS LTD.
Trafford Catalogue #00-0070   www.trafford.com/robots/00-0070.html

10   9   8   7   6   5   4

Cupid's Secret is a true story written by a farmer who saw something special in a little horse that no one wanted. See how a chain of events changed this little horse's life after they met.

Dedication

This book is dedicated to Alexi Page who was born blind and had a deep fear of horses. Today she has overcome those fears and has fallen in love with a horse in this book. My prayer for her is that she will someday see the horse that she has come to love and ride.

And a special thanks to her mother Bo, who discovered Trafford Publishing whose staff assembled this story into a book.

Thank you to Mom, Ruth, Trish, MaryBeth, Sharon, Barb, Kim and Megan for your editing input. Thank you, Lisa, Gail, Cheryl, Debbie, Sharon, Kate, Shaun, Tracie, Joe and Jessica, for the care you give to Cupid and Arrow along with the other 87 horses at Hillside Equestrian Meadows.

Cupid's Secret

FARMER BUCK LOOKED AT HIS WATCH. "Good," he thought. "It's only four o'clock. I still have plenty of time to fix this broken fence and make it to the horse auction by seven." He liked going to the auction. As he busily repaired the fence, he reminded himself that he really didn't need any more horses. Ninety horses were certainly enough and he had no intentions of purchasing any horses that night.

The auction had already started by the time he arrived. Some of the sale horses were show horses, and others were work horses. Some were former family pets that were no longer cared for and others were so sickly that no one dared to buy them.

Farmer Buck walked through the large auction barn. Many horses were standing in closed pens, like big cages with barely enough room to walk around or lie down. He looked at the horses and noticed how some of them tried to get his attention. "Pet me, I'm a good horse" said a black horse silently as he nuzzled Farmer Buck's hand. "Wow you're a beauty," said the farmer to the proud looking black thoroughbred. "Don't you know it!" said the horse to himself. Farmer Buck noticed a matched pair of work horses standing together in a large stall and said, "You guys don't look too happy." "Ha!" they both thought. "Would you be happy if you knew that tonight you'd be separated from your best friend? Someone who you have played and worked with all your life? We're only here because our owner died and no one can care for us any longer."

In the next pen stood a small sickly horse. She was brown with a black mane and tail and stood with her back toward the farmer. He noticed that her ribs protruded through her skinny frame. Gently he kicked some hay into her pen. She turned and sadly glanced at him. "Poor little horse. She's probably too frightened and sick to eat," he thought.

"You hoo, over here," neighed a fat little pony. "Don't look at that ugly thing. Look at me. Bet you don't know why I'm here," he whinnied. "I wish I could tell you how a little boy hit me with a stick. When I kicked him, he told on me. I'm really sweet though," continued the pony whose eyes pleaded for attention. But Farmer Buck did not understand. He continued past the little pony and looked for an empty seat inside the crowded auction area.

It was getting late and by ten o'clock many horses had already been sold and were on their way to new homes. Some of the fancy show horses sold for thousands of dollars. Some of the young horses sold for only hundreds of dollars because they still needed training. There were so many horses, all sizes, dispositions and colors. Nice family horses were sold to other nice families, or at least they hoped so.

Some of the horses seemed confident and pranced proudly in front of the many onlookers. Others seemed frightened by all the noises coming from the large gathering of people. "I should probably buy some of these horses," thought Farmer Buck. But he quickly reminded himself that it was winter and all of the stalls were filled back at his farm.

The auctioneer introduced horses by their numbers and announced their selling prices into his microphone and the loud speakers

carried his voice above the noise of the crowd. "Now entering #345, a 7-year-old registered Golden Palomino," he said. The elegant horse proudly carried his rider in front of the interested crowd. "Sold," he announced and pointed to its highest bidder, an excited woman with a kind face. She held up her bidder's number to record the sale and hurried excitedly from her seat and hugged her beautiful new horse.

As the last few remaining horses waited their turn to be introduced by the auctioneer, a little skinny sickly brown horse was led into the auction arena by a young girl. Farmer Buck recognized her as the one he had kicked hay to and noticed that perhaps she wasn't being ridden because she was too thin to carry the weight of a rider. "Or maybe she was never taught to carry a rider," he thought. The little horse sadly hung her head when she heard the auctioneer make fun of her skinny frame. Her long bangs thankfully covered the tears she was fighting to hide.

"The poor thing," he thought as she was led in front of the thinning crowd. No one bid on her. No one wanted her. She glanced at Farmer Buck. "Please, won't you buy me?" she whinnied weakly. "She's talking to me," he thought. Farmer Buck knew he shouldn't buy another horse but she lifted her head and exposed a white heart-shaped marking on her forehead. "Is she trying to tell me something? Does she want me to buy her?" he wondered. "Is she showing me her beautiful heart-shaped marking to get my attention?"

Just then, he heard the auctioneer yell "Sold." Can you guess whose hand was up in the air? Farmer Buck had purchased the little horse for $325.00. He followed her back to her pen and looked at his new horse. He moved his hand toward her forelock to brush it aside, when suddenly the frightened horse jumped away from him. "It's okay," he gently whispered. "You look like you need a second chance in life. I have a feeling that the kids on my farm will give you that chance." "I've heard that before," she thought sadly to herself. Farmer Buck said good night to his new little horse and promised to return the next day and pick her up.

The following morning he arrived at the auction barn with his big truck and shiny trailer. He found the little brown horse standing in her pen. She had been patiently waiting for him, anxious to leave the overwhelming sights, sounds and smells of the auction barn. Her frightened eyes bulged and protruded from her frail face. She appeared uncertain as to what was happening and yet inwardly she hoped that her new home would be a kinder place to live than the ones she had come from. Farmer Buck softly spoke to her and offered her a carrot. He knew how much horses loved carrots but she would not eat it. "She doesn't trust me," he thought.

He led her to the trailer and cautiously she followed. She stood quietly as the trailer door closed behind her. "Where is he taking me," she wondered. He placed hay nearby so that she could eat during the long drive to her new home. But the little brown horse was too nervous to eat. "Hang in there," he whispered to her. "No one is going to hurt you. You'll see. You're in for a real treat."

But the little brown horse was too weary to believe him. She concentrated on maintaining the strength she needed to remain standing during the haul to the farm. Her stomach ached, she needed rest, and she worried that "I'm not what this farmer thinks I should be. He's not going to be happy once my secret comes out," she thought.

The farmer pulled the truck and trailer into the long driveway leading to his big farm. Curiously the horses grazing in the large pasture ran to the fence to see who was arriving. "Is he bringing home a fancy show horse or perhaps a pretty little filly?" said Cody, the herd's ringleader. "Oh, I hope it's a friendly horse," said Frisco who didn't like horses that played roughly.

The kids on the farm ran to greet the trailer. Some of them lived in the city and visited the farm on weekends. Others stopped by during the week after they had done their homework. Farmer Buck liked sharing his horses with the kids. He enjoyed seeing the smiles on their faces as they learned how to care for and skillfully ride his horses.

The big trailer door opened and there stood the frightened little brown mare. She trembled and stared back at the many faces peering in at her. The children's faces, once filled with anticipation and smiles, changed quickly to surprise as they saw the sickly-looking horse for the first time. They asked Farmer Buck why he had brought this horse to the farm. They were kind children and were used to the usual traffic of new horses that often arrived at the farm. It was winter, she's sick, you can't ride her, the stalls are filled. "What was the point?" they asked. "Oh, there's a point," thought the little brown horse. "That's my secret," and she prayed to keep it.

"Gather round, kids," called Farmer Buck. "This little horse needs some loving. She is weak, skinny and scared. She needs to trust us. I think something has gone wrong in her life. Maybe she was abused. Can you believe she refused to eat a carrot from my hand?" "Maybe she was in the

care of someone who didn't understand her," said one of the kids. "Maybe she is a wild horse," said another. "Regardless of what her past may have been like, it is time to undo whatever is frightening her. Let's give her a chance to have a bright new future. I'll need your help," he said. "Oh, you can count on us," said the kids.

They watched as Farmer Buck gently reached toward her fore-locks. She raised her head. "Easy girl, easy," he said. "I'm not going to hurt you." He gently brushed her forelocks aside and exposed the unusual white mark on her forehead. "Wow!" exclaimed the kids. "That's a perfect heart," they said.

"What shall we call her?" he asked them. The group fell silent as each began to think of a name that would suit her. Farmer Buck's young nephew Ryan said "Hey, it's almost Valentine's Day and she does have a perfect heart on her forehead. Let's call her Cupid." "Cupid, yeah!" every-one cheered. Farmer Buck agreed that it was a wonderful name and so it was that the little brown horse was named Cupid.

"Cupid looks terrible," one of the boys said. "Well, she certainly needs to be bathed and groomed. Let's make it our job to help her feel special. Maybe then she will lift up her head and feel good about herself.

Who wants to help?"asked the kind farmer. The kids all raised their hands. A plan was put into motion.

Cupid was quarantined and put into a small barn all by herself. "I'm so glad to be in this cute little barn by myself," she thought. "I don't want to infect any of the kind farmer's horses." Her runny nose and mangy fur told the story of her ill health. She rested snuggly in her stall, grateful for the rest and solitude. It had been a long day and Farmer Buck had his workers check on her several times a day. She was given medicine, plenty of food and water and a medicated bath that cleaned her fur of the fungus that caused her fur to smell badly and her skin to itch.

Throughout the next two weeks, Cupid rested comfortably and carefully observed those who cared for her. "They seem kind enough," she thought. " Maybe I can trust them with my secret." "No, not yet," she reasoned. "I still don't know them well enough."

Cupid rested quietly in her stall and small paddock area where she stepped out daily for a little exercise. The workers who checked always brought along a carrot which they offered to her from their hands. Cupid would sniff the carrot and appeared interested, but never once did she eat one. "How strange," they thought. "She won't eat carrots from our hands, but when we leave them in her dish she gobbles them up!" Cupid wanted to trust them, but she wasn't yet brave enough to risk eating from their hands.

One morning as Farmer Buck prepared Cupid's breakfast, one of the barn kids asked if he could help feed her. "Sure," he answered. When Cupid finished her breakfast of pellets and hay, the farmer suggested that Brian try and pet her face. "I know she doesn't trust adults. Let's see how she responds to you," he told Brian. Brian approached Cupid and slowly reached his hand toward her face. Cupid stood still and did not appear nervous. In fact, she seemed to enjoy her cheeks being patted by Brian's gentle hands. "Wow!" said Farmer Buck. "Look at how she trusts you. I was right. She must have been mistreated by adults." The farmer was an experienced horse handler and instinctively knew that Cupid was ready to be trained. And he knew that he needed the kid's help if her training was to be a success.

The next day he gathered some of his best students and explained his theory about Cupid's fear of adults. He outlined how he wanted her training schedules to be followed and asked the boys if they felt up to tackling what appeared to be a difficult rehabilitation project. Thirteen-year-old Shaun spoke up first. "Oh yes. I definitely want to help." The others pledged their support too. Cupid's training was ready to begin.

Kyle, at twelve years old, was already an experienced horse handler. He placed a halter on Cupid's head and secured a lead line to it. Shaun showed her a saddle. Ryan placed a saddle blanket on Cupid's back and then took the saddle from Shaun. He gently placed it over the saddle blanket and balanced it carefully on the little horse's back. Ryan grabbed the dangling girth strap and began to tighten it around Cupid's belly. Her eyes began to bulge and instantly she began to buck. "Hold on, Kyle!" yelled Farmer Buck. "Get out of the way boys." Cupid continued bucking as if she were a rodeo horse. She grunted and bucked, and bucked and grunted. She wanted that saddle off her back!

Kyle could not hold her any longer. Farmer Buck climbed over the fence and quickly took the lead rope from Kyle before Cupid could run away. He loosened the girth strap and the saddle slipped off Cupid's back. Almost immediately she stopped bucking and stared at Farmer Buck. "Did he just help me?" she wondered. "If he did, this would be the first time an adult did something nice to me." She took a step closer to him and relaxed as he gently patted her neck. "See Cupid, no one is going to hurt you. That

14

was just a saddle we placed on your back. You'll be all right," he reassured her. Cupid seemed to understand and her bulging eyes softened encouraging him to keep petting her. "Hmm" she thought. "That feels good."

Farmer Buck picked up the saddle and showed it to Cupid. "See," he said. "It's just a little saddle. No big deal." She stood quietly as Shaun first placed the blanket pad and then saddle on her back. He slowly tightened the girth and this time, instead of bucking, she remained still, standing very close to Farmer Buck. "Please take it off," she pleaded with her nose that lightly nudged his hand. But the saddle stayed on and Cupid accepted it as something the kind farmer wanted her to wear.

Farmer Buck walked Cupid around the arena. "Hey," she thought. "This saddle isn't such a big deal. It actually feels quite nice even though it feels tight on my belly." They walked together for a while longer and were pleased with her acceptance of the saddle. He had Ryan take the saddle off and everyone agreed that Cupid's first saddle lesson was a good one. She seemed to understand that no one, including the saddle, was going to hurt her.

All the boys gave Cupid a gentle pat and Farmer Buck reached into his pocket and offered her a carrot. She wiggled her nose to see what he held in his hand but would not eat the carrot. He bent over and placed it on the ground, let her loose and then walked away. Cupid watched him and the boys leave the area. When they secured the gate, she let out a big "Neigh," and happily ate the carrot. "Good-bye," said the boys. "Tomorrow is another day," said Farmer Buck. "Remember boys, you can't do too much with her all at once. Her training must be done in small, little accomplishments so she won't feel overwhelmed. We'll try something else tomorrow."

The next day, Farmer Buck and Ryan went into Cupid's pen. She watched them put the saddle on the fence. "Uh oh," she thought. "They're going to try to put that on my back again." She began to run around her little paddock. Ryan followed as he tried to catch her. Cupid ran into her stall. "Thank goodness," she thought "my stall door is always open. I'll just hide in here." "Thanks Cupid," said Ryan as he caught up to the quick thinking mare. "You just made my catching you a little bit easier," he said as he closed her stall door. Slowly he walked toward her and gently put on her halter. "Come on girl. Let's see if I can sit on your back," he said as he led her from her stall. "It's time for your next lesson." Cupid let out a big snort.

Farmer Buck held her lead rope as Ryan brushed and groomed

her. "I think Cupid likes this," he told his uncle. "Her fur is beginning to look healthy and even has a little shine to it." Ryan was ready to put the saddle on Cupid's back. He gently placed the blanket on her back and positioned the saddle on top of it. "Talk to her Ryan as you tighten the girth," suggested his uncle.

Cupid remained calm as the saddle was placed on her back although she curiously turned her head to smell it. Just then Shaun arrived. He was riding his horse Thunder and Cupid noticed how happy they both looked. "But doesn't his horse mind carrying that boy around on his back?" wondered Cupid. Suddenly, Farmer Buck had an idea. "Shaun, why don't you bring Thunder over here and let Cupid see you ride him. Maybe it would help her understand that it's okay for a rider to sit on a horse's back and she'll accept Ryan on hers," he said.

Thunder was a stocky horse with a great attitude. He was given to Shaun last year as a gift from Farmer Buck who realized that Thunder needed someone to love and care for him. Shaun fell in love with Thunder from the moment the brown gelding first arrived at the farm. Shaun and Thunder made a beautiful team and Cupid watched as Shaun dismounted and kissed his horse on the nose. Cupid noticed that Thunder smiled. "What a happy team," she thought.

"Come on Ryan, get on," she heard Farmer Buck call to his nephew as he petted her. Cupid prepared herself and easily accepted the saddle. "Hey," she thought. "If Thunder can do it, so can I." Farmer Buck petted her and spoke reassuringly that everything would be okay as Ryan lightly placed his foot into the stirrup and then slowly eased himself into the saddle. "Hold on," warned his uncle. "Here we go," thought Ryan.

Ryan held his breath and Cupid's eyes turned toward his uncle. She was looking for reassurance and Farmer Buck could see her moving her ears back and forth. Cupid focused on Ryan and then on the farmer. She looked over at Thunder who said, "Hey little girl, it's okay. These guys are cool. They aren't going to hurt you."

Cupid began to walk. Her pace quickened as she adjusted to Ryan's weight and leg pressure. "This isn't so bad," she thought as she slowly began to relax. After a short while Farmer Buck told Ryan to dismount. "That's enough for today," he said. "Let's take the saddle off and give her a rest." Shaun removed Thunder's saddle too and the two horses moved toward each other in a friendly manner. "How nice," thought Farmer Buck. "Cupid saw how well Shaun treated his horse and how much they love each other. Let's give these two horses a chance to chat and get acquainted. We'll check on them in a little while and see how they're getting along," he said.

Farmer Buck approached the pair and petted Thunder on the neck. "You are a wonderful horse, Thunder. I love how kind you are to Shaun," he said as he took a carrot from his pocket, placed it in his hand and offered it to the horse. Thunder quickly ate it. Cupid watched with amazement. "Wow!" she thought. "Thunder didn't even hesitate to take that carrot from his hand. I wish I had his confidence." Just then Farmer Buck turned toward her and offered her a carrot too, but she only sniffed it. He placed it on the ground for her and turned to leave. She watched him walk through the gate and Ryan and Shaun followed. "The coast is clear," she thought as she turned to eat the treat he had left for her. "Where is it?" she wondered. She spun around, searching with her eyes and probing through the loosely packed dirt. "Where is it? I know it's here somewhere." But it was gone. Thunder had already helped himself to it. His cheeks looked like stuffed squirrel cheeks as he chomped his extra treat. At that very moment Cupid learned a valuable lesson; if one doesn't accept something nice that is offered, someone else may want it and take it before there's a chance to reconsider.

The following day the boys asked if they could get Cupid ready for her next training session. Farmer Buck agreed and reminded the boys to follow the training schedule. Shaun went to get Thunder while Kyle and Ryan went to catch Cupid. Linda, one of the kids from the barn was invited to watch Cupid's training session that day. She hoped to one day work as a trainer and enjoyed watching training sessions.

About an hour had passed when she went running into the barn calling for Farmer Buck. "Quick, quick," she yelled to him. "You have to see this." He followed her and passed Cupid's empty pen. The gate was open and no one was around. At first he worried that she might have gotten out but then Linda pointed toward the distant hill leading to the wooded trails. "Look she cried." He recognized Shaun and Thunder riding along the hill top but could not make out the horse and rider that followed. "Who is that?" he asked looking at their silhouettes in the distance. "That's Cupid," said Linda. "Ryan is riding her." Farmer Buck felt some tears welling up in his eyes. He was no longer nervous that Cupid wasn't in her pen. He was delighted that she was on her way to a new experience.

Cupid was enjoying herself. She didn't mind carrying Ryan on

her back and was fascinated with the many new sights they explored together. When they returned to the barn, Farmer Buck asked Ryan how Cupid responded to her first trail ride at the farm. "She was fine," said Ryan. "She did whatever Thunder did. I think she likes him." The boys removed their saddles and brushed their horses. Linda led Cupid outside and brought her to an area of tall green grass that grew outside the wooden barn. Cupid took of few bites of the sweet clover and smiled as she looked around at her lovely new home. "How lucky I am to bring my secret to this wonderful farm."

In the distance Cupid could see a riding arena where some horses were being ridden in English saddles. Some were jumping, some were cantering and all of them moved like elegant show horses. Linda gazed at Cupid and wondered what she might be thinking. She began to talk to her. "You know Cupid, maybe you could do that if you really want to. You see, I'm a lot like you. Six years ago I came here on a school trip and saw a lot of new things that really interested me. I couldn't afford the cost of lessons but from that day I dreamed of one day being able to ride. Farmer Buck saw my interest and invited me to the farm on weekends. Sometimes, when I didn't have a ride, he drove to my house in the city and picked me up so I could help out at the farm. I loved working in the barns and have learned a lot. He taught me that with hard work and desire I could ride and show horses. There were days when I was tired and hated work and even thought about quitting. But I would return home, see my friends hanging out on the streets and getting into trouble and I knew I wanted a better life for myself. I've seen many horses do well here and you could do well here too." "It's all up to you. Do you want a better life for yourself?" she asked Cupid. "If you do, you're at the right farm."

Cupid listened as Linda spoke to her. Cupid did want a better life. She wanted a much better life and felt lucky that she had been pointed in the direction of this amazing farm opportunity. But she wasn't yet ready to expose her secret. And so neither Linda, Farmer Buck nor the kids knew what secret she was keeping.

Summer arrived and the farm was alive with kids and riding lessons. Cupid's training was at the point where she enjoyed being in the big show barn. She would stand quietly and let the kids brush her. She was familiar with the many people who worked at the farm and the lessons she was expected to learn. Yet no matter how hard she concentrated on what she was doing, her thoughts usually drifted onto something else.

One day Nicole, a young girl who worked on the farm, went to Farmer Buck and asked if she could use Cupid for a lesson. Nicole was teaching a little girl named Kate how to ride. "Do you really think you can trust her with a beginner rider?" he asked. Nicole said, "Yes." "I've been working with her and I believe she would be patient with my student." "Okay," he agreed.

The following day Cupid entered the indoor arena and joined the other lesson horses. They gave her a quick once-over and went on with what they were doing. Word traveled quickly throughout the farm that Cupid was in the lesson arena. The farm kids curiously poked their heads in to watch her lesson. So many people had played a part in helping the little horse adjust to the farm and they proudly watched her helping a young child learn to ride. The little girl sat tall in the saddle and Cupid held her head up high as she slowly walked around the arena. The little girl finished her lesson and Nicole led Cupid back to her stall. "She is the most beautiful horse here," said the little girl to her mother. "What?" said Cupid to herself. "Me, beautiful? She must be joking," thought Cupid. "Nicole, please can I ride Cupid next week?" begged the little girl. "Me?" questioned Cupid. "Someone wants me above all the other horses to choose from? Someone wants

me?" With that she galloped off toward the barn whinnying, "I'm wanted, I'm wanted, someone wants to ride me." Cupid remembered Linda's words of encouragement. Cupid had made up her mind that she was going to become the best lesson horse on the farm. And she did become the best by far.

By the end of summer Cupid became one of the farm's favorite lesson horses. She was used for English lessons and jumped low fences carrying students proudly on her back. One day, Cupid overheard some of the show horses talking about a big upcoming fall English show. Kimberiah, a sixteen-year-old show horse owned by Gail, the farm's English instructor, said, "I hope the jumps are big because that's how I like them. I jumped higher than five feet at my last show in Florida," she boasted. Blanco, a beautiful gray thoroughbred bragged that he would be groomed to perfection and have all the spectators wooing over him. "Remember," he proudly declared, "I'm the only horse here that had my pictures taken by a famous Grand Prix photographer." Jaguar, owned by Farmer Buck's daughter, said she felt proud to carry young Michelle throughout the show. Each horse in turn talked about having their manes and tails braided and about who would be riding them in the show. All the horses, that is, except Cupid.

The following week little Kate came for her lesson. She read the notice on the barn's bulletin board about the Hillside Equestrian Meadows fall horse show. As Nicole prepared Cupid for her lesson, Kate asked Nicole if she could show Cupid in some of the classes. Cupid listened in amazement. "Me? Kate wants to ride me in the big English show? Can I do it?" wondered Cupid. Instantly her thoughts drifted to when she was last in front of so many people. It was at that awful auction. She thought about how far she had come since then. She thought about Linda's story and how Thunder took her carrot. This was an opportunity to prove herself worthy. Not only to everyone who helped bring her to this point but mostly to herself. Suddenly Cupid felt special, secret and all!

Over the next few weeks Cupid and Kate practiced often. Cupid learned to correctly jump small fences. Sometimes she would hit her legs on the rails and it would hurt. But then she would remember next time to lift her legs a little higher. There was so much to remember. Stay straight. Move consistently. Canter on the correct lead. As the show neared, Cupid prayed that she would be ready. She practiced and practiced. She would not let the other show horses' comments discourage her. Sometimes they would laugh at her, especially when she would hit a rail. But Thunder was always there to remind her not to pay attention. "Just do it for yourself," he would say. Cupid liked Thunder. He supported her dream of becoming a show horse. He understood that she wanted to be a show horse more than anything else. Of course she wanted it for herself. But she still had a secret and she was doing it for that too.

On the day of the show Cupid awoke very early. The weekend workers arrived before sunrise and she could hear them roll the grain cart down the concrete aisle way delivering breakfast to each awakening horse. Kate and Nicole arrived and gave Cupid a bath and then beautifully braided her mane and forelock. Cupid enjoyed all the attention and liked being pampered. She appreciated hearing the many compliments about how beautiful everyone thought she looked.

The outdoor jump arena had been groomed to perfection. The jumps looked beautiful. Some looked like brick walls, and others like stone. Some had boxes filled with pretty flowers and others were painted with bright bold colors. Horse trailers arrived bringing elegant show horses and their well-dressed riders. Moms and Dads brought their kids, crowds of spectators found seats in the viewing areas and excitement filled the air.

The riders were dressed in proper English attire. Saddles and bridles were oiled and clean. Kate made some final adjustments as she saddled Cupid. Before mounting she kissed Cupid on the nose. "It's my first show too, Cupid. I'll do my best and I know you'll do the same. I just know you'll be perfect," she said. "Oh no," thought Cupid. "I'm counting on you to help guide me and make me look good."

Kate mounted Cupid and they began to warm up. They trotted up the hill and passed Mari, a city girl who works on the farm every weekend. "Good luck, said Mari. Thunder whinnied, "You look great Cupid. You go girl!" They reached the show ring and trotted around. Cupid looked at everything. The man on the loud speaker reminded her of the auction and she froze. "What's wrong?" asked Kate as she gently patted her neck. Cupid relaxed and continued to trot. Another announcement, "Five minutes till show time." Cupid knew the time had come. "I can do this," she reassured herself. "I have to." She set aside her fears and memories and concentrated on Kate's cues.

"Ladies and Gentlemen, please stand as we salute our flag," said the announcer. As the Star-Spangled Banner played, Cupid's thoughts drifted to how happy she felt to be part of this special day. She was happy that she brought her secret to this loving home where she was surrounded by kind friends who treated her well. "If my special day ended here and now," she thought "it would be enough to satisfy me." But Cupid did not realize that her special day was just about to begin.

The first class was called. Many horses and riders entered the arena. Cupid watched from outside the fence and paid special attention to how each horse carried its rider. She wanted to learn as much as she could before her class was called. She listened for their class to be called and finally heard the announcer say, "Short Stirrup riders please enter the arena. We're looking for the following entries: #22 Alexi riding Brandon, #19 Danielle riding Houdini, #27 Katie riding Misty, #31 Marilyn riding Darwin and #22 Grace riding Coolie and #32 Kate riding Cupid."

"Well, this is it," thought Cupid. "Here we go," said Kate as they excitedly walked into the arena. The horses looked well-groomed. Cameras flashed, parents waved. It was very exciting. "Trot please," called the announcer. Kate pressed her heels lightly against Cupid's sides near the girth. Cupid quickly responded to Kate's request for the trot. Kate picked up the correct diagonal and Cupid proudly trotted along the fence. When she passed Farmer Buck, she heard him say, "You look good there, Cupid." Cupid smiled. "Thank you, Farmer Buck. Thank you for noticing me," she thought.

Cupid loved being in the show arena. She felt special. She felt beautiful. She felt important. She paid close attention to Kate's cues. "Wow!" thought Cupid. "This is hard." But they were well prepared for the different commands they were asked to perform. "All riders halt," said the announcer. "Line up and face the judge."

The judge, Mrs. Jensen, was a tall woman with a kind face. She carefully reviewed each horse's performance. "Okay Cupid," said Kate, as the judge approached. Kate cued Cupid to stand perfectly still. Cupid understood the cue and responded correctly. She stood perfectly still and did not move a hoof. Mrs. Jensen carefully moved down the line and inspected each horse. Cupid was proud of herself and knew that she had tried her best.

Finally the judge had made her decision and handed the results to the announcer. "Ladies and gentlemen," the announcer's voice bellowed, "all of today's riders did very well." Kate felt pleased and patted Cupid on the neck. "And," he said, "the judge has awarded first place, the blue ribbon to Number 32 – Kate who is riding Cupid." The crowd applauded. Kate bent down and hugged Cupid. Shaun, Ryan, Kyle, Linda and Mari, along with everyone else who knew Cupid, let out a victory cheer. Some began

to cry, not sorrowful tears, but tears of joy.

Thunder heard the announcement from his paddock and let out a big whinny. Cupid was in shock. The many hours of hard work had certainly paid off. "If I didn't win," she thought "I'd still be a winner for having the courage to make it this far." Farmer Buck walked toward the arena gate and waited for Cupid and Kate to exit. "Nice job," he said as he reached up and patted Cupid's neck.

Everyone from the barn was waiting to congratulate them. Parents and friends snapped photos and she received lots of hugs and kisses. Cupid sensed their love and joy and contentedly she smiled. Cupid looked at the kind farmer who was petting her neck. He held a carrot in his hand that he had saved for her. "Here Cupid. Here's a little victory treat for you," he said as he slowly moved his hand toward her mouth. "Thank you Farmer Buck," she thought as she nuzzled his hand and took the carrot from him.

"This is the happiest day of my life," said Kate "and I owe it all to Cupid." "Wow!" thought Cupid as a tear fell from her eye. "That's just what I was thinking." Cupid realized that although these people were her friends, if she had shared her secret she might have missed being a part of this special day. "I'll just have to keep it to myself a while longer," she thought. What kind of secret was Cupid keeping?

That night Cupid lay down in her soft fluffy stall. Kate had placed the blue ribbon on her stall door and it hung proudly above Cupid's nameplate where everyone who passed by could see it. "Nice job today Cupid," said Blanco. "I was proud of how well you did today," commented Kimberiah. Thunder whinnied from his stall across the barn yard, "You showed 'em all Cupid. Good night," he said. "Good night everyone," said Cupid. "Thanks for making me feel welcome." Cupid prayed and thanked God for a wonderful day.

Thanksgiving Day arrived. Cupid felt healthy and looked well-rounded. In fact, she looked a little too well-rounded. Farmer Buck thought she had gained too much weight and considered changing her food rations. "Oh no," thought Cupid. "I can't hide it anymore. I have to tell someone but who, and how?" Cupid decided to share her secret with Thunder.

One day as they passed a sunny, lazy afternoon resting in the big field by Farmer Buck's house, Cupid asked Thunder if she could share something special with him. "Sure," he said. "You know you can tell me anything." Cupid began to speak just as a trailer drove into the driveway. "Who is that?" asked Cupid. "Oh, that's someone who's come to buy one of

Farmer Buck's sale horses," he said. "Where will he go?" she asked. "I don't know, but the new owners seem like nice people," he said. "You see, Cupid, every Thanksgiving season Farmer Buck tries to find good homes for his summer lesson horses. That way he doesn't have to send them back to the auction."

"Will I be sold?" she asked. "I don't think so," he said. "You seem to be one of his favorites and you're useful. As long as you pull your weight around here you'll probably be able to stay." "Thunder," said Cupid. "I must tell you something special. I'm in foal and I will soon be delivering my baby." "You're what?" cried Thunder. "You heard me," she answered. "But no one knows yet. I was very skinny when I was brought here and naturally everyone thinks that my weight gain is from the healthy food I've been eating. What will happen to us when I have the baby and Farmer Buck realizes that I can no longer be ridden while I nurse my baby? Do you think he'll sell my baby? Do you think he'll sell me?" she asked. Thunder did not know how to answer or reassure his friend. "I will keep your secret. I don't know any other way to help you." "Oh Thunder, your friendship is all the help I need right now. You're the best friend I have ever had."

On Thanksgiving day Cupid said a little prayer. "Dear God, I know there must be a point as to why I'm living on this wonderful farm. I pray for your continued help that will point me in the right direction and give me the strength I need to safely deliver my baby. You are all-knowing and I pray our futures will point us to life on this farm forever. Amen."

Winter began to move in and the stalls filled up fast. Farmer Buck and his family prepared for his annual post-Christmas vacation. Cupid thought, "I must keep this baby a secret until he leaves. I don't want to interfere with his vacation plans." Cupid knew how much the kind farmer needed some time away from the demands of the large farm and that he would want to assist her during the delivery. "I simply won't disrupt his plans," she thought. "I'll just have my baby when he is on vacation." She carefully lowered herself into the cozy bedding of fluffy shavings in her stall. She rested comfortably and smiled as her unborn foal gently kicked from within. "Yes, my little one. Be patient. We must wait a little while longer, she said as she lovingly glanced at her rounded belly."

On Christmas morning Farmer Buck fed the horses and started the long list of morning chores. He enjoyed giving his hard-working staff this special day off. "Merry Christmas Brandon," he called to his oldest and most favorite horse. He slid open Brandon's stall door. The statuesque chestnut gelding moved toward him and nuzzled the farmer's cheek. Brandon, a fourteen-year-old Quarter Horse was an amazing horse and together they were one of the most successful gymkhana teams on the show circuit. Farmer Buck was a highly skilled rider and coupled with Brandon's blazing speed and athletic ability, they were always in the winner's circle. Brandon could do it all: English, Western, speed, pleasure, jumping, trail rides, therapeutic riding for disabled children and adults. Brandon's incredible accomplishments earned him the position of leader among the herd. He was respected and admired by all the horses and by everyone who rode him.

Farmer Buck reflected for a moment on their first meeting so many years ago at the very same auction where he had purchased Cupid and other remarkable horses. Brandon was then a handsome two year old. The farmer had a keen eye for special qualities some horses have and immediately recognized Brandon's athletic potential and unique disposition. The youngster was intelligent and quickly learned some tricks that through the years delighted hundreds of people. Farmer Buck taught him how to shake hands, and answer questions with an affirmative shake of his head and of course, everyone's favorite, how to play "dead" on a cue. "Merry Christmas old boy," he said as he lovingly rubbed Brandon's ear. "Here's a delicious apple for my special friend." "Brandon stood proudly and accepted the treat from his favorite rider. He loved Farmer Buck very much and enjoyed their annual Christmas morning time together. "Thank you," he thought. "It is a privilege to be your personal favorite. You can always count on me to safeguard your herd and safely carry your student riders" he said as he whinnied to his special friend.

Farmer Buck gave Brandon one last hug and securely closed his stall door. "The others are waiting," he said to Brandon as he opened the next horse's stall. He continued to feed the horses and reflected on each one as he tossed two flakes of sweet hay into their feeders. He thought about each one; from where each had been bought, about the good job each had done on his farm and about the pleasure they had brought to the many different riders they carried.

The large doors to the barn slid open. "Merry Christmas Farmer Buck," called Shaun who arrived pulling a sled of apple-filled baskets. "I'm planning to give these Christmas treats to all the horses," he said. "I can see you're well prepared," said the farmer as he looked at all the apples on his sled. Shaun jumped on Thunder and grabbed the sled's rope. Thunder liked pulling the sled. They headed off toward the upper barn with the baskets

securely in place on Shaun's sled.

There were almost ninety horses at the farm. Some of them lived in little shelters and others lived in stalls inside the different barns located throughout the 50-acre property. Shaun and Thunder stopped at each barn and made sure every horse received a Christmas apple. "Look Thunder," said Shaun. "There's plenty of apples left. Let's give an extra apple to those horses in the outdoor shelter. I feel a little sorry that they don't have a cozy stall." Thunder laughed quietly to himself. "Shaun," he thought. "I wish I could ease your mind and tell you how much we like living outdoors, even in the winter. As long as we have shelter, food and water, we're fine."

As they continued down the outdoor path Thunder noticed that Cupid was in an outdoor shelter. "Hey Cupid," he said. "Why are you out here?" "I guess Farmer Buck needed my stall for that new horse from Florida who arrived without a winter coat of fur.," she answered. Thunder looked at his friend and asked, "Are you okay out here?" "I'm fine," she reassured him. "If you saw my other homes, you'd understand why I'm happy living anywhere on this wonderful farm. At least here I am fed and properly cared for."

"But Cupid," he said. "You will need an indoor home for your baby. We've got to get you back inside," he insisted. Cupid knew he was right and Thunder could see the worried look in her eyes. "What's the point?" she asked. "Oh there's a point all right," answered Thunder. "You'll see, there'll be a point to all of this, I just know it," he said. "Thunder, there's nothing I can do right now. Indoor stalls are valuable and I'll have to manage out here."

That Christmas evening Cupid prayed. "Dear God, is there a point to my baby being born in the middle of winter? I pray you will keep a watchful eye and protect my baby from harm." Cupid nestled in the fluffy bedding Shaun made for her and rested comfortably as she felt her baby moving. "I just know there must be a point to all of this," she thought as she drifted off to sleep.

It was late in January when Farmer Buck left for his Florida vacation. He had worked hard all year and everyone knew how much he needed a restful break. "How kind of him," thought Cupid "to move me back into an indoor stall before he left. I'm glad that I could help that needy horse from Florida during her stay with us."

Soon after the farmer left, Cupid knew the time had come to

deliver her baby. "Everything is in place," she thought. Her indoor stall was cozy and a soft snow fell lightly outside. She would wait until everyone was asleep and knew she could hold her labor off until then. She prayed one more time. "Dear God, when I first came to this farm I had no talent and I was not pretty. I was ill and had no one to care for me. Thank you for bringing Farmer Buck into my life. Thank you for pointing him to my pen at the auction. Please point my baby in the right direction too, so that he will one day be worthy of being noticed. Point him to the path of health, success and happiness. Amen."

Everyone was asleep. The barn was dark and still. Cupid lay down as the birth process began. Her stall was warm and cozy. How she wished that Thunder and her other friends could be there to support her. "Ouch," she moaned as her foal's brown legs appeared. "Ooh," she groaned as its nose and little head arrived. Cupid lovingly looked at her newborn son. "A little colt," she thought. "How lovely."

His mane was black, and she thought he was the most beautiful colt she had ever seen. She watched him carefully as he lay at her side, and she smiled as he began to breathe his first breaths of life. He had arrived safely.

"Thank you, God," she prayed.

Cupid was tired and wanted to rest, but she had work to do. "I'm a mother," she thought "and I must clean my beautiful little son." She licked his ears and then his nose. She cleaned him all over and then nuzzled him. "Come on, stand up," she said softly. "You need to get up and drink some milk to keep you warm and healthy." The newborn colt tried to lift himself up, but his spindly legs were unsteady and he could not stand. "Come on. Try again," encouraged his doting mother. "You can do it." "Okay Mama," he said. "I'll try."

With all of his might and determination the little colt pushed and pushed until he was finally standing. "Mama, I think I figured this standing thing out," he said proudly. But his little legs wobbled and "plop," he fell down. "Oops," said the little colt. "I guess I spoke too soon. Watch me try again, Mama." Cupid smiled and watched patiently as he once again attempted to stand up. He pushed and he pushed until he was finally standing. He wiggled and he wobbled and with great determination said, "Look Mama, I'm standing up." The little colt carefully balanced himself and when he was confident that his legs would cooperate and stop wobbling, he took a step toward his mother.

Moonbeams filtered through the barn windows and into Cupid's stall. They landed on her newborn son and gave her the light she needed to look at him clearly. "What a fine-looking colt you are," she said as she gently stroked his neck. The little colt smiled and turned toward his mother's milk sac to drink his first meal.

Cupid watched as he took his first taste of her milk. Her eyes traveled down his neck and across his back and then in amazement froze when they reached his little rump. Her eyes fixed on a triangular patch of white fur. "Huh?" she thought. "Is that a birthmark or is the light playing tricks on me?" she wondered. She nudged the spot with her nose and carefully licked the large patch of fur. She lifted her head to view the area again and knew at once that God had heard her prayers. She realized the point to all of this after all.

The large white patch of fur that lay across the colt's rump was a perfectly formed arrow. Cupid knew that the white mark on her forehead was the point of attraction that helped Farmer Buck notice her at the auction. Her white mark had saved her and now her son had a white mark as well. Cupid smiled knowing that it was the point she had prayed for. Surely he would grow up to have a life as wonderful as hers. The newborn colt poked around his mother's belly and helped himself to another meal. "Drink up," she said. "It's cold outside and the milk will help keep you warm." "Okay Mama," he said and continued nursing. Finally with his belly full, he laid back down. Cupid took her place by his side and knew her body heat would help keep him warm. As they cuddled together, she could feel the warmth from his little body. She smiled contentedly, knowing that in spite of the freezing temperature he was warm and cozy.

Cupid was tired. She gazed at her sleeping son and knew that finally she could rest and take a nap. She was anxious to share her good news with Thunder and her other friends but realized it would have to wait until tomorrow. She knew how happy they would be for her and sensed that Farmer Buck would be happy too. "Thank you God," she prayed. "Thank you for everything." She gently placed her head over her sleeping son. "Good night my little boy," she said softly. "Tomorrow will be a big day for us; I will finally let everyone in on my secret and you will meet the world."

The End

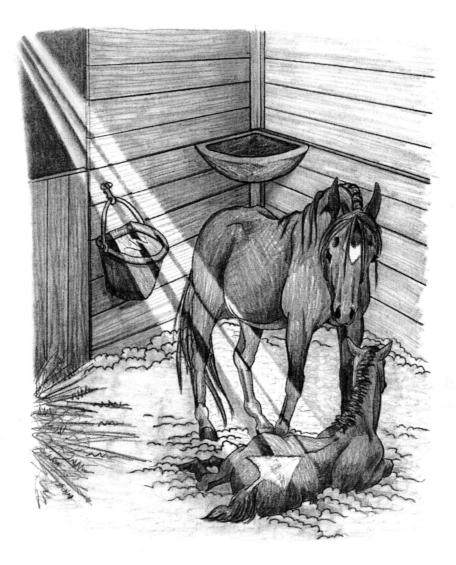

CUPID'S SECRET

GLOSSARY OF TERMS:

1. **Auction** - a place where people bring horses to show and sell to the highest bidder
2. **Bridle** - the leather head piece that holds the bit in the horse's mouth and reins to steer the horse in the direction you want to go
3. **Colt** - a baby male horse
4. **Diagonal** - a term meaning rhythm of rider trotting English.
5. **Filly** - a baby female horse
6. **Foal** – a baby horse
7. **Girth** – a strap or leather belt that is used to hold a Western or English saddle in place
8. **Gymkhana** – games played on horseback to test the skill of the rider and horse as a team.
9. **Saddle** - the leather seat that is strapped to a horse's back. It is designed for a person to sit on with stirrups to put your feet in. It is placed on top of a blanket or pad on the horse's back and secured by the girth.

10.**Stall** - An area 10 feet by 10 feet with a door and window for a horse to eat and sleep within a barn. Keep it clean and they will love you for it.

ISBN 155212406-1